Mrs. Lovechild

The Fairy Spectator

The invisible Monitor

Mrs. Lovechild

The Fairy Spectator
The invisible Monitor

ISBN/EAN: 9783337227135

Printed in Europe, USA, Canada, Australia, Japan

Cover: Foto ©Andreas Hilbeck / pixelio.de

More available books at **www.hansebooks.com**

THE VISION.

THE
FAIRY SPECTATOR;

OR, THE

Invisible Monitor.

BY

Mrs. *TEACHWELL*

AND

Her FAMILY.

London:

PRINTED BY AND FOR JOHN MARSHALL NO. 4,
ALDERMARY CHURCH-YARD, BOW-LANE;
AND NO. 17, QUEEN-STREET, CHEAPSIDE.
1790.

To Mifs *M----*.

My DEAR,

I DEDICATE this little book to you as a token of affection.

Were I a Fairy I fhould devote much of my attention to you. Had I the Bonnet which Mifs *Child* prudently declined accepting, I fhould be frequently at your elbow: but if I were in poffeffion of the wonderful Ring which was offered to her, I fhould, probably, fometimes conceal myfelf from your fight, for the friendly purpofe of remarking your conduct when

you

you suppose yourself to be unob-
served: and I hope that I should
have the pleasure to see you act
always, as if you were in the pre-
sence of your dear Mamma; or,
to speak in still higher terms, as
if you remembered that *there is
an Eye which sees us wherever we
are.*

These are *my* thoughts: now
I will tell you *yours.*

You think, that if you had
such a pair of Looking-glasses as
those which were placed in Miss
Child's closet, you would consult
them on every occasion; and always be careful to act in a becoming manner.   You

You think, that any little girl, who had Mifs *Playful's* Rofe, would be moft exceedingly circumfpect in her behaviour.

You think, that with Mifs *Child's* Locket, you fhould furely never be guilty of a fault.

Let us ftrive to improve thefe thoughts, by doing what is in our power.—I will endeavour to improve you by admonition, though I cannot drop from the bell of a Lilly to attend you. Do you make the beft ufe of the opportunities of improvement you enjoy; which, (though not fupernatural) are great; for though

no

no Fairy watches over you, you
are bleft with one of the beft of
mothers! That her care for you,
and the reft of her children, may
be bleffed with fuccefs, is the
fincere wifh of,

My dear,

Your affectionate friend,

E------ F---.

THE

THE

CONTENTS.

(No. I.)

FAIRY SPECTATOR.

—◆—

The DREAM.

—◆—

ONE morning Miſs *Sprightly*, inſtead of riſing the moment ſhe was called, burſt into tears, and complained that ſhe was awakened from the moſt pleaſing dream which ſhe ever had in her life.

Mrs. *Teachwell* inquired whether ſhe was ſick, that ſhe was ſo ſlow in riſing?

Madam, ſaid ſhe, I beg your pardon, but I cannot baniſh the thought of my dream.   Idle

Idle girl! replied Mrs. *Teachwell,* make hafte!

When the young ladies were running and playing in the garden, Mifs *Sprightly* was found in a corner of a room in tears.

Mrs. *Teachwell* accofted her with great good-humour, faying,

My dear, what ails you?

Mifs replied,

Madam, I am forry and afhamed; I thought fo much of my dream that I could not attend as I ought to do to my prayers.

Mrs.

Mrs. *Teachwell* anfwered,

My dear! I hope that your for-
row will produce amendment; you
muft lay afide all other thoughts
when you pray.

Madam, faid Mifs *Sprightly*, I ftrive
to do fo, but I never can forget this
dream.

Silly child! exclaimed the Go-
vernefs, go and play; among your
companions you will foon lofe the
thought of fuch folly.

Mifs *Sprightly* courtefied, and was
going out of the room, in obe-
dience

dience to Mrs. *Teachwell*'s commands, but her air was so pensive, that the good lady called her back; and tapping her shoulder, asked what this dream was, which dwelt so long upon her thoughts? then, bidding her sit down, indulged her wish to relate what had passed in her mind, which she did in the following words:

‘ I had been reading in *Gay's Fables*; and as the evening was very bright, I took the book into my chamber; after I was in bed I read *The Mother, Nurse,* and *Fairy*; and I believe that I dropped asleep with the book in my hand.’

But

But your dream? interrupted Mrs. *Teachwell.*

Madam, said Miss *Sprightly,* you shall hear. I thought that I was sitting alone in that pretty summer-house where I once drank tea with you, as a reward, because I came of my own accord to tell you that I chanced to break the looking-glass which hung in our chamber; and as I was amusing myself in observing a very fine dragon-fly, I was surprized with the sound of the softest, sweetest music that I had ever heard; at the same time the most delicate perfume seemed to proceed from the wings of the fly: I was all wonder; yet how did my surprize increase, to

B   see

fee the wings of the infect fpread into
a loofe robe; and the little creature
itfelf change to a woman no bigger
than the fmalleft wax doll. Oh dear!
fhe was fo very pretty, that I could
have looked at her all day: at laft
fhe fpoke.

I am, faid fhe, a Fairy. I am your
guardian, to watch over your mind;
although you never faw me before,
yet I have always feen you. I have
known every action, every word, nay,
every thought.

I fmiled and was going to fpeak,
when fhe interrupted me; and, pul-
led out of her pocket two of the
prettieft looking-glaffes that ever were

seen,

seen, she extended her hand; I reached to take them, and that moment I awoke. Miss *Friendly* was at my bedside, calling me to rise, else I should have tried to fall asleep again, in hope—I see you smile, Madam; but indeed I would have given my week's allowance to have recovered my dream.

(No. II.)

FAIRY SPECTATOR.

———

The CONVERSATION.

———

MRS. *TEACHWELL*, who is indulgent to every innocent wish, which can be directed to any good purpose, told Mifs *Sprightly*, that she would continue her dream, that is, said she, I will write you a dialogue, in which the Fairy fhall converfe; and I will give you a moral for your dream.—— You know that ftories of Fairies are all fabulous?

Mifs SPRIGHTLY.

Oh yes! Madam.

Mrs.

MRS. TEACHWELL.

Do you wish for such a Fairy-guardian?

Miss SPRIGHTLY.

Very much, Madam.

MRS. TEACHWELL.

Why, my dear?

Miss SPRIGHTLY.

Because she would teach me to be good; for I should be ashamed to have even a naughty thought.

MRS. TEACHWELL.

I love you for your earnest wish to be good—but tell me, is not every action, word, and thought known?

Miss SPRIGHTLY.

To whom, Madam?

MRS. TEACHWELL.

Consider!

B 3

Miss

Miſs SPRIGHTLY.

I know whom you mean, Madam.

[Mrs. TEACHWELL.

Well, my dear, are you not afraid
to indulge a naughty thought?

Miſs SPRIGHTLY.

I did not conſider this before; for
we are apt to forget what we do not
ſee.

Mrs. TEACHWELL.

Remember, that He, who ſees all
you do; who knows all you ſay, or
think, will either reward you if you
be good, or puniſh you if you be
wicked.

' God, who ſeeth in ſecret, himſelf
ſhall reward thee openly.'

Company coming in put an end to Mrs. *Teachwell's* stay in the room, and Miss *Sprightly*, retiring to her own chamber, wrote as follows in her memorandum book.

- May I always consider that God is every-where present; that He knows all which we do, say, or even think; and oh! may I always strive to please Him!

In the afternoon Mrs. *Teackwell* called Miss *Sprightly* to her: she ran with beating heart, hoping that her good Governess had written the dialogue, but it was only to give her some directions respecting her work. The little girl was rather disappointed,

but

but she said to herself, my dear Mrs. *Teachwell* is very kind to promise me so much pleasure; and I ought not to trouble her with impatience, but wait her leisure, rather than teize her with inquiries when she will gratify my curiosity.

The next day Miss *Sprightly* was called to read the following story:

(No. III.)

FAIRY SPECTATOR.

The MIRRORS.

SHEWING

What we are,

AND

What we ought to be.

STORY of Miss CHILD.

WRITTEN AT THE REQUEST OF MISS SPRIGHTLY,
BY HER FRIEND, E. TEACHWELL.

STORY.

MISS *Child* had the misfortune to lose her mamma when she was but five years of age. She was put immediately under the direction of a governess: this lady was genteel in

her

her appearance, and pleasing in her
manner; had a fashionable address,
and appeared to be at least *not* un-
accomplished; these external advan-
tages misled the judgment of some
of her acquaintance, who overlooked
her deficiency in more material points,
and recommended her to Sir *Thomas
Child*, as a person well qualified for
the important office of educating his
daughter.

It is easy to suppose that the attention of such a governess would be
engrossed by outward accomplish-
ments. Miss *Child's* person and dress
appeared to great advantage, and her
father being either to indolent, or
too busy to inquire further, flattered

himself

himself that she improved very fast, and applauded the choice to which his friends had directed him.

But alas! the poor girl's mind and temper were neglected; so that she grew proud, selfish, peevish, and vain.

Miss had a closet which Lady *Child* had taken delight in fitting up for her, in a manner suited to her age. There were toys to amuse her, and such books as she was capable of understanding. There were *The Good Child's Delight*; *Little Stories for Little Folk*; *The History of Little Boys and Girl*; and many other entertaining and instructive little books,

such

such as were suited to her tender
age.*

These little books had cuts in them,
which drew the young lady's attention at first; but they were soon laid
aside, and the useful lessons which
they contained forgotten.

Her ladyship's intention was, as
her daughter advanced in years, to
have removed the childish toys, and
those first books, and to have filled
the

---

* Since the writing of this, many very
pleasing books have appeared, which would
have made a most agreeable addition to
Lady *Child*'s Library for her daughter on
the projected plan.

the shelves with such volumes as were adapted to the more improved state of her mind.

Happy in the idea of seeing her daughter's progress, she had provided a *series* of books for her use, to be produced as she should have occasion for them; but her death put a stop to the improvement which she had planned; and the closet remained as childish a place as when the owner was really a baby.

Miss had an allowance for her pocket expenses; she kept no account, neither was any inquiry made how the money was expended, nor advice given how she ought to dispose of it.

C   The

The governeſs carried her pupil conſtantly to the dancing-ſchool, where ſhe met a great many genteel children. Exceeding pains were taken that her coat ſhould be made in the moſt faſhionable manner; her cap be as ſmart as that of the firſt young lady there; but this care ſtopped at appearances.

A ſtranger would often ſay; ' Miſs *Child* is a fine girl!'—but no body replied to that ſtranger, ' ſhe is an amiable girl!'—Nay, ſome could not refrain from ſhaking their heads, and ſaying, ' it is a pity that her mind ' is not as agreeable as her perſon.'

(No. IV.)

FAIRY SPECTATOR.

Story of Mifs CHILD continued.

The CLOSET.

ONE day Mifs *Child* was fitting in her clofet; fhe was engaged in looking over a box of feathers and artificial flowers, in order to make choice of fuch as fhould be moft becoming to her complexion.

As fhe waved her head to admire herfelf in the glafs, fhe faw the reflection of a very beautiful female looking over her fhoulder: fhe ftarted,

C 2   and

and turning about, called out peevishly,
—Who are you?

FAIRY.

Your guardian.

Miss CHILD.

One governess is enough for me.

FAIRY.

I am the guardian of your mind;
I know all your thoughts.

Miss CHILD.

What do I think now?

FAIRY.

That you neither desire nor need
such a director.

Miss CHILD.

Bless me! it is true. What was
I thinking when you came in?

FAIRY.

That you would buy a larger look-

ing

ing-glass to hang in your closet; now
I have brought———

(producing something.)

Miss CHILD.

O dear! what are they?

FAIRY.

Two mirrors.

Miss CHILD.

For me?

FAIRY.

If you please——take this.

Miss CHILD.

(looking in the glass, exclaims as she
throws it down.</i>)</p>

Frightful!

FAIRY.

(picking it up, holds it to Miss Child,
who, seeing her own image again re-
flected, exclaims, with emotion.</i>)</p>

C 3 Worse!

Worfe! I look uglier than I did before.

FAIRY.

That is because you are in an ill-humour; you are angry at having your faults obferved.

Mifs CHILD.

Certainly I am! Who is not?

FAIRY.

Now look in the other glafs.

(*holding it up.*)

Mifs CHILD.

Charming! oh, give *this* to me.

FAIRY.

I will give you both.

Mifs CHILD.

I will not have *that*——take it away; it made me appear fo hideous!

FAIRY

FAIRY.

You *shall* have both; if it be not your own fault you will appear agreeable in each. These are ENCHANTED GLASSES: *one* shows you as you *are*, the *other* as you *might* and *should be*; but they are best explained by examples, which I will give you; first making known to you the character of the persons who have had them in possesfion. I shall begin with Miss *Pettish*.

(No. V.)

FAIRY SPECTATOR.

PEEVISHNESS *and* PRODIGALITY.

PEEVISHNESS.

FAIRY.

MISS PETTISH was so ill-tempered that every person hated her; till, by the use of this pair of glasses, she reformed her disposition.

You are to observe, that I insist that my pupils shall write an account of what passes, as they find it in the mirrors; this is to be done journal-

wise,

wife, in two oppofite pages of the fame book.

The firft day that Mifs *Pettifh* had the mirrors, this was the account, by which you will find that the reflection of your image in *one* glafs fhows your difpofition; in the *other*, teaches you how you ought to behave.

This then is Mifs *Pettifh*'s account from her appearance in the *Firft Glafs*, which fhows things *as they are*.

' My new cap, made by Mifs *Modifh*, was awry; I found fault with it, and though Mrs. *Fancy*, my mamma's woman, faid in excufe, that fhe had juft received a letter, acquainting her

that

that her sister was dangerously ill;
and that her distress at this melancholy intelligence occasioned the mistake; yet I pouted, complained, and
would have it altered immediately.'

SECOND GLASS.

Showing things as they ought to be.

' I should have merely observed civilly that there was a little mistake in
the cap; and when I had heard the cir-
cumstance which occasioned it, I should
have considered how concerned poor
Mrs. *Fancy* must be at the melancholy
account of her sister, that it was exceedingly obliging in her to attend
at all to my dress in such a situation;
and I ought to have begged of her to
think

think no more of such trifles on my account : nay, I should have told her, that I would requeft leave of my mamma for her to vifit her fifter."

PRODIGALITY.

Mifs *Lavifh* fpent all the money which she received as foon as she had it ; she fancied herself *generous,* becaufe it fometimes happened by chance that an object fell in her way, juft as fome perfon had given her money ; and in that cafe she parted from it without thought, and went to her papa an hour after for more. She likewife thought that she was *charitable,* becaufe she was willing to give away whatever halfpence she might

happen

happen to receive, to the firſt poor child whom ſhe met.

But ſhe never would ſacrifice the ſlighteſt whim of her own, to enable her to relieve the actual wants of another.

She never parted from any thing to gratify a little friend, unleſs when ſhe was tired of it herſelf.

She kept no account of her expenſes; but when ſhe was aſked how ſhe had ſpent the laſt money, uſed to reply, ' indeed I do not know, it is gone!'

Nay, ſometimes, if ſhe wanted

money in her Papa's abfence, fhe would borrow, and often forget to pay.

In her own opinion, and that of a few filly inconfiderate people, Mifs *Lavifh* was, as I have faid, of a noble difpofition, *generous* and *charitable*.

You find that fhe was not *juft*; but that never entered her mind.

How would fhe have ftartled to be told that fhe was *mean, felfifh, covetous*; perhaps fhe might not have blufhed at being called *extravagant*; which fhe was with refpect to herfelf, but niggardly to others.

(No. VI.)

FAIRY SPECTATOR.

CAPRICE;

O R,

The CAPRICIOUS GIRL.

Miſs Laviſh's account of her expenditure
of money on reflection.

MY Papa made me a preſent of
money to expend as I liked on my
birth-day.

I bought a ſuit of the new ſpang-
led ribbons and a fan; theſe coſt
all my guinea, except half a crown,
and

and that was not quite enough to buy the pocket glafs for which I wifhed, fo I afked for fome more money. He gave me half a guinea. As I went out to get the glafs, for which I was very impatient, a poor woman came to the door; I wifhed that I had had fomething for her, as fhe feemed to be almoft ftarved, and I afked both the fervants whether they had any money; but they could not lend me any. Away we drove— As I paffed through *Holborn* I faw a man who fold birds; I then changed my mind, determined to wait for the glafs, and purchafe a bird. For this I gave five fhillings. I then drove to the next ftreet to get a cage. I was obliged to give half a guinea

D 3

for one, which was gilt, fit to hang
in my dreffing room; this was half
a crown more than I had; but the
man civilly offered to truft me for
that.

*Mifs Lavifh's confcious recollection of what
fhe ought to have done.*

I fhould have gone to the poor
widow, whofe hufband was killed laft
week in the gravel-pit, and have
given her fomething to enable her
to buy bread for her five fmall
children.

I fhould not have turned away in
a huff when *Betty Broom* faid to me,
' Mifs! the price of one yard of that
ribbon

ribbon would keep poor *Mary Need* from ftarving;'—but have thanked her for reminding me of my duty.

I fhould not have afked my papa for more money, unlefs it had been for a much better purpofe; and I fhould have given him an account how I had expended his bounty.

I fhould have inquired who the poor woman was, whom I met at the door: I fhould have informed myfelf how fhe was circumftanced, and have applied a part of my half guinea in the relief of her family.

I fhould on no account have con-tracted a debt.

I fhould

I fhould have been contented with
a plain cage—the price of that which
I bought would have clothed a poor
child.

Now, faid the Fairy, to Mifs *Child,*
you underftand how thefe glaffes may
improve you—make a proper ufe of
them.

Look in *this*—nay, never ftart;
you muft firft fee your faults, before
you can mend them. To me you
appear juft as deformed without the
glafs, whenever you are ill-difpofed,
or act unworthily.

I will hang the glaffes here. Pro-
mife me that you will confult them

every evening; they will bring to your recollection the tranfactions of the day; they will inftruct you how to judge of your actions. Record in this book the report of the glaffes; on one leaf *what you are*; on the oppofite, *what you fhould be.* Adieu!

　　　　So faying, the Fairy vanifhed.

(No. VII.)

(No. VII.)

FAIRY SPECTATOR.

REFORMATION.

As soon as the glaffes were placed, and the Fairy gone, Mifs *Child* furveyed her clofet, in order to obferve how the mirrors appeared as a part of the furniture.

As fhe caft her eye upon the firft glafs, fhe remarked that her little prints and toys, with the number of looking-glaffes, had a very pretty appearance, and fhe herfelf feemed like a great wax doll in a baby-houfe.

Well,

Well, faid fhe, I look very fmart! and my dolls and all my play-things look very pretty in the glafs; this is like having two fets of toys.

Turning her head to furvey the clofet, fhe caught a glimpfe of the fecond glafs, which fhowed *what ought to be.*

In that fhe faw a girl like herfelf, dreffed with great neatnefs, yet in a plain and modeft manner. This phantom took down all the childifh toys, and diftributed them among a number of little people, who ftood around, fmiling and thanking her for making them fo happy.

She

She ftood looking very earneftly,
and foon after fhe faw this figure
take all the little books off the fhelves,
and give them to the children; after-
wards the looking-glaffes, and laftly,
the little coloured prints.

Mifs *Child* then faw her likenefs
fill the fhelves with another fet of
books. She could difcern, *Birth-day
Prefent*; *Sunday Improvement*; *Courfe
of Lectures for Sunday Evenings*; and
feveral other little volumes — then
Mrs. *Chapone*, Mifs *Talbot*, and many
more authors of whom fhe had never before heard the names.

A ftandifh and paper next appeared
upon the table, which was before
                                    ftrewed

ftrewed with rags of gaufe and fnips of ribbon. There ftood too a work-bafket, with fciffars, thimble, needle-book, and thread-papers. The young lady feated herfelf, and took out a piece of fine old cloth, cut out a little fhirt, and began to work.

Blefs me! faid Mifs *Child*, I dare fay that the linen is for fome poor little babe—I have feen many who were almoft naked: oh! that I had made fo good a ufe of my time!

Juft as fhe fpoke, her friend the Fairy appeared.

Mifs courtefied, and returned thanks for the glaffes; but alas! faid fhe, they

they make me miserable; becaufe they convince me, that I am very different from what I ought to be.

Shame for paſt faults, ſaid the Fairy, is the firſt ſtep towards amendment.

I feel ſhame enough for my folly, exclaimed Miſs *Child*; alas! I am only a great over-grown baby; my perſon and limbs have ſo got the ſtart of my mind, that I bluſh at myſelf.

Your regret, ſaid the Fairy, at your want of improvement, muſt be a ſpur to your future diligence; ſince you are conſcious of ignorance, and deſirous defirous of knowledge, application will foon repair your loft time.

But my difpofition is as unculti-vated as my underftanding ; I have no command of my temper; no re-gular mode of action ; caprice and paffion govern me.

My dear, faid the Fairy, I am charmed to find that you have the difcernment to fee your faults, and the humility to own them. I will affift you in the neceffary work of reformation.

(No. VIII.)

FAIRY SPECTATOR.

———◆———

The L O C K E T.

———◆———

MISS *Child* was fo diffident of herfelf, that fhe perpetually fummoned her friend the Fairy to afford her an opportunity of converfing with her on the fubject of her conduct.

One day, when the amiable girl had difcovered an unufual degree of modefty, the good Fairy produced a fmall cafket, took from thence a Locket,

Locket, set with pale rubies, and presented it to Miss *Child*.

Madam! I thank you, said the young lady; but I had rather be excused from excepting your present; had it been a book which would instruct me in your absence!—but an ornament to wear!—no, Madam! I am too vain already : pardon me.

This, replied the Fairy, is not such a trinket as will increase your vanity: wear it constantly about your neck. You see that it is of a delicate pink colour; the hue will vary as your disposition changes.

If you feel envious, one of those
rubies

rubies will turn to a dirty yellow.
If you be angry, that ftone will glow
like fire; if you be foolifhly timid,
that lower ftone will become white;
fhould you be niggardly, thefe points
will have a dull blackifh hue, and
jealoufy will turn the whole locket
to a colour like that of a common
pebble in a gravel-pit.

Thus explained, faid Mifs *Child*, I
fhall rejoice to wear the ornament, and
accept it with exceeding thankfulnefs.

By degrees this young lady acquired
every good quality with which her
friends could wifh to fee her endowed.

The laft virtue which fhe gained,
was

was that active benevolence which seeks to discover the wishes of another in order to gratify them.

I mentioned the toys and little books being removed from her closet, but did not say what became of them—they were thrown promiscuously into a chest, and laid by disregarded and unthought of. One day it occurred to Miss *Child*, what pleasure they would afford little people to whom they were suitable.

Immediately she sent for several of her young friends and acquaintance, whom she introduced into her chamber. She received them with so much condescension and kindness, that they

were

were quite charmed with her; she
regaled them with a treat, compofed
of fruits and cakes; talked with them
of their improvement, and, in fhort,
fhowed every mark of attention and
civility that fhe could think of.

Before they left her room, fhe
prefented each with a fmall token of
affeftion, fuited to their refpeftive
ages, from among the toys and little
books with which her clofet had been
filled.

The children were all delighted,
and jumped and danced round her
with joy and thankfulnefs.

Now, faid fhe; thefe little treafures
give

give me more real fatisfaction than they ever did formerly, even when they were fuited to my years. How much better, continued fhe, is this, than to hoard up what was of no ufe to me, and proves fo agreeable to my little friends! I never faw any object fo pleafing as this little group of happy beings fmiling upon me! So faying, fhe caft her eye upon the Locket, which hung in her bofom, and was furprifed to fee it glow and fparkle like coals when they are blown; reflecting at the fame time, all forts of faint and beautiful co-lours, like a fine diamond.

Blefs me! exclaimed fhe, this is an appearance which I was not taught to expect; I wish I could see the charming Fairy—surely nothing is amiss!

She then dismissed her little visitors with civility and gentleness; they could not cease to talk of the change in Miss *Child.*

' How gentle she is! how obliging! how generous! said the little people as they retired.'

(No. IX.)

(No. IX.)

FAIRY SPECTATOR.

The GIFTS.

As soon as Mifs *Child* was left alone, fhe went into her clofet to confult the mirrors; and to her unfpeakable fatisfaction fhe found, that her image appeared the fame in both; for fhe was now become *what fhe ought to be.*

The Fairy entered, and expreffed her fatisfaction at what had paffed. You were furprifed, faid fhe, at the glowing appearance of your Locket;

you

you had not been apprifed of that,
nor could you have conceived an idea
of the complacency attending a con-
fcioufnefs of doing well—of obliging
and pleafing by acts of beneficence,
till you had experienced it.

Mifs *Child* returned abundance of
thanks to the good Fairy, and en-
treated that fhe would never forfake,
but continue to watch over her. I
am now, faid fhe, fenfible how un-
fit I am to guide myfelf. The Fairy
affured the charming girl of her
protection, and grew more familiar
and frequent than ever in her vifits.

Mifs *Child* became fo perfectly
amiable, that fhe was the darling of her
guardian

guardian Fairy; who one day made her an offer of the following gifts, out of which she might choose one.

A *Purse*, which she should always find full of money.

A *Bonnet*, that would convey her to any place of which she should think as she put it on.

A *Ring*, which would make her invisible.

Miss *Child* acknowledged her obligation to the Fairy for her offer; but said, that she was fearful to accept such gifts.

If,

If, added she, I had a Purse which would always be full of money, I might not make a proper use of it, or, even if I did not spend it in an improper manner, yet I should at least lose all merit in giving to my friends or the poor; since I could be neither *generous* nor *charitable*, if I had not myself the *less* for what I gave.

Had I the Bonnet which would convey me instantly to any place where I might wish to be; though it appears to me that I should be very happy in the power of flying to assist my friends, or relieve any person in distress; yet I will not presume too much; I should probably sometimes

convey

convey myfelf for purpofes lefs important, and lefs amiable, from a place where I might have been employed in doing kind offices, which my duty required.

For the Ring—I dare not accept that on any account. Should curiofity ever tempt me to liften to a converfation which was not defigned for me to hear, I fhould be very culpable, and, perhaps, gain no fatisfaction; for even if what I heard were agreeable, my heart would reproach me with the crime of prying into the fecrets of another perfon; and fo deprive me of that pleafure which I now enjoy, if I hear myfelf praifed; when I hear *fairly* what paffes.   F   The

The Fairy embraced her, and said,
Now, my dear, I am convinced of
your prudence. I made this trial of
you with trembling; **for** though we
know the prefent thoughts of our
wards, yet we cannot be certain what
they will be on occafions which may
arife. You have withftood fuch a
temptation as I fhould not have ven-
tured to place before you, but that
I had a high opinion of your dif-
cretion; yet I could not with pro-
priety have given you the reward
which I propofed, without making
this trial; from this time you fhall
be my companion; no longer called
Mifs *Child*, but *Amiable*, and your
employment fhall be fuch as I know
will be very agreeable to you—I ap-
point

point you guardian to the little people in Mrs. *Teachwell's* family; to
form their difpofitions, and regulate
their conduct—For this purpofe I will
endow you with the power of affuming
what fhape you pleafe, a privilege
which I am confident you will only
exert for excellent purpofes.

(No. X.)

FAIRY SPECTATOR.

The DOLL.

ONE morning, when the school-bell rang for breakfast, Miss *Playful* not appearing, Miss *Friendly* fought for her throughout the houfe and play-ground, and, at laft, found her fitting alone in an arbour, in the moft remote part of the garden. She had in her hand a doll; and was fo bufily engaged in dreffing it, that fhe neither faw Miss *Friendly* enter, nor heard her fpeak, but kept prattling to the wax baby in her lap.

Hey

Hey day! faid Mifs *Friendly*, are you there? what brought you fo far from the houfe?

I will tell you, faid Mifs *Playful*: this is my new doll, which Lady *Lovewell* fent me: and I took it into this clofe walk, becaufe I had a mind to drefs it alone, left any of the young ladies fhould interrupt me; for really, when one has any thing new or pretty, they throng about one fo that there is no comfort in playing with it.

And was not this very felfifh in you? faid Mifs *Friendly*; would you have liked that *Mary Freewill* fhould have ferved you thus, when her new

toys

toys came? or do you think fhe would have done fo? you may recollect that the dear little girl, when her baby-houfe came, did not give herfelf time to unpack her whole fet of furniture till fhe had called you—' *Polly*, faid fhe, will like to fee the things as they are taken out.'

The little girl blufhed, and made no reply—but was very attentive whilft Mifs *Friendly* continued fpeaking. I am very forry, my dear, you fhould fo far forget yourfelf, as to neglect this opportunity of obliging your friends; what fatisfaction could you have in hiding yourfelf in a corner? and what joy would it have been to a good-natured girl, to affemble

thofe

thofe young ladies with whom fhe was intimate, and make them fharers in her pleafure! How differently would *Amiable* have counfelled Mifs *Child* to behave!

Indeed, faid Mifs *Playful*, I am afhamed; but I have no Fairy to advife me: as fhe faid thefe words, they reached the door of the break-faft-room. Mifs *Friendly* obferved the behaviour of the little girl at her entrance: much furprife was expreffed at the abfence of *Polly*; a thoufand encomiums beftowed on the doll; the beauty of her face, and the elegance of her drefs delighted the little peo-ple in general; and feveral of them expreffed a wifh to play with it a

little

little while, and affift in undreffing it.

Mifs *Friendly* thought this **a fa-**vourable opportunity for conveying a leffon in an agreeable manner : fhe remarked all that paffed on this oc-cafion, and others which arofe in the courfe of the day; and the **next** morning prefented Mifs *Playful* with a paper, containing a narrative of the morning tranfaction, and a con-verfation *fuppofed* to have paffed in the arbour between herfelf and the Fairy *Amiable*, whom fhe is feigned to have feen in a vifion.

(No. XI.)

(No. XI.)

FAIRY SPECTATOR.

The V I S I O N.

A Little girl, whofe name was *Playful,* had a prefent made her; it was a nice wax doll: the morning after fhe received this treafure, fhe rofe very early, ftole flily to her drawers, and packed the doll, and all her cloaths into a fmall work-trunk: thus prepared, fhe waited with impatience till the time for the young ladies taking their morning walk, and feized the firft opportu-

nity

nity of running unperceived along
a clofe walk which led to an arbour,
where fhe thought fhe could amufe
herfelf with the doll, unobferved by
her fchool-fellows.

With beating heart fhe unlocked
the trunk which contained the object
of her joy; feated herfelf on a bench,
and placing the doll by her fide, felt
in her pocket for a pincufhion.

A bird flew into the arbour; alight-
ed upon a branch of jafmine clofe at
her elbow, and hopped about, finging
all the while. She forgot her doll,
and fat filent with pleafure.

Prefently the bird flew away; fhe
then

then turned about to look at the doll, and saw her arm move: surprised, she exclaimed, 'Are you alive?'—I am, said the doll, but be not frightened. No, indeed, said the little girl, I am not afraid; for I have done no harm, nor do I mean to do any; but this is strange!—she said no more; when

Thus spoke the doll:

'My name is *Amiable*; the good Fairy, who, as you have heard, watched over my conduct, when I was a girl like yourself, has bestowed upon me some privileges annexed to fairy-hood. One of these privileges is the power of assuming any shape which we please, with this restriction; that

we

we cannot injure thofe who are *good*
in *thought*, *word*, and *deed*; nor can
we even frighten them.—Now, you
were **not** perfectly free from fufpi-
cion of a flight fault, fince your coming *alone* into this corner, with your
new doll appeared felfifh : I thought
that this fault might make you liable
to a flight punifhment, and was fearful that your furprife at my fudden
appearance might become your punifhment; though I did not wifh to
inflict any.'

'No indeed,' replied the little girl,
' I fay my prayers conftantly; in them
I afk to be freed from *fear* as well
as *danger*, and I feel confident of
fafety.'

' You

' You charm me, my dear: did you obferve the bird which flew into the arbour ?'

' Yes, it was a fweet little crea-ture !'

' I was the bird : had you fpoken to me, I fhould have converfed with you in that difguife—as you did not, I took this fhape, as being familiar to your eye, and agreeable to your fancy; but now I will appear in my fplendor.'

Down dropped the doll.

Soft harmony breathed through the fluttering leaves—gales of perfume

G were

were wafted all around; the flowers
feemed to glow with livelier tints:
Mifs *Playful* fat in filent expecta-
tion, when, from the bell of a white
lilly, defcended a human figure, ma-
jeftic, though fo fmall, and graceful
beyond any mere mortal being;
cloathed in a loofe, flowing mantle,
ample, and falling in elegant folds,
fhe appeared ftately like the queen
of Fairies on a court day: yet her
garment, though it feemed fo full,
did not conceal the beauty of her
figure, which was fo delicately form-
ed, that defcription can give little
idea of it. Upon her head fhe wore
a coronet of diamonds, emeralds, and
rubies.

Mifs

Miss *Playful* gazed and smiled; but said not a word: when, behold, this little creature vanished, and in her place appeared a female of still more exquisite beauty: her robe was light as air; if I were to compare it to any thing terrestrial, I should say that it resembled purple gauze, and silver gauze, folded together; and purple brilliant gauze; and it fluttered like the garment of an air-nymph. Her lovely hair was bound with a wreath of the most delicate flowers.

Smiling, she said, " You see here a specimen of my power; I can vary my appearance at pleasure; but I came on an errand of importance: See here !"

G 2

"I have brought you a Rose; place it in your bosom; it will adorn and delight you; but it has a Thorn, which you will feel whenever you do amiss."

"I must now haste away. I see you part from me with regret; but I will soon return. Whenever you are desirous of seeing me, rub the green leaf of your Rose (*thus*) gently with your finger. Adieu!"

(No. XII.)

(No. XII.)

FAIRY SPECTATOR.

The ROSE.

———— " a pigmy fpright
" Popt through the key-hole, fwift as light."

GAY.

MISS *Playful* took an early opportunity of fummoning her friend
the *Fairy*, who inquired how fhe liked
the flower?

Mifs PLAYFUL.

I like the Rofe, but not the
Thorn.

FAIRY.

I told you that it had a Thorn:—
I hope——   G 3   Mifs

Miſs Playful.

It has never wounded me much;
yet often makes me ſtart without rea-
ſon. If it were only to prick me
when I am really naughty I ſhould
not complain; but it ſtings me when
I am not to blame.

Fairy.

Tell me an inſtance of this.

Miſs Playful.

Soon after you left me I ran in to
eat my breakfaſt, and I felt the Thorn
as I entered the room.

Fairy.

Your little heart exulted with pride.

Miſs Playful.

The young ladies aſked me a great
many queſtions about my doll; I
took pleaſure in anſwering them; and
all

all this time I smelt a delicious perfume from my Rose.

FAIRY.

Very well.

Miss PLAYFUL.

But when Miss *Pert* told me that
I was too big to play with a doll,
and that it was babyish in me to
carry it about, I felt the Thorn;
yet I said not a syllable.

FAIRY.

But you felt angry?

Miss PLAYFUL.

I did indeed think she was rude.

FAIRY.

You have not told me all now—
your Rose reproved you for a little
envy, when Miss *Trifle* produced her
new buckles; and for some vanity in
showing your fan.   Miss

Miſs PLAYFUL.

I am ſorry to find, that I am not
ſo free from naughty paſſions as I
thought I was.

FAIRY.

My dear, ſelf-knowledge is hard
to attain: if you make a proper uſe
of my flower it will render you a
moſt amiable girl.

I know you, and will ſhow you
to yourſelf without flattery. You difcovered ſome wiſdom in being willing
to ſubmit to the hints of the Roſe;
and, by the accuſation which you urge
againſt it, (that the Thorn pricked
you without juſt cauſe) you only prove
the need you have of ſuch a monitor.

Miss PLAYFUL.

Pride, envy, and vanity!—Who would have thought that I had such evil difpofitions!—I am quite unhappy to have been fo miftaken in my opinion of myfelf—I thought that I was free.

FAIRY.

Be not difcouraged: the wifeft perfons may err in judging of themfelves. Do you patiently fubmit to endure the rebukes of your bofom friend: turn them to your advantage, by ftriving to correct the beginnings of every evil paffion, and you will be delighted with the beauty and fragrance of my Rofe: for if you be as good as you can be, the flower will look frefh and beautiful, and fmell delicioufly; but

it

it will abate in delicacy of hue and
fcent whenever you tranfgrefs; and
you know from experience, that every
time that you fwerve from your duty,
even in thought, you will feel pain in
confequence of your fault; but I muft
further tell you, that in proportion
as you were to blame, the Thorn would
wound you—will you venture to wear
it?

Mifs Playful.

Certainly, I will.

Fairy.

Were you to tranfgrefs materially,
the Rofe would fade proportionably
to the greatnefs and frequency of
your faults; and if you were to be
incorrigible (which heaven avert!)
the flower would wither, and feem

to

to die ; it is, however, really immortal, and would in time revive to torment you.—Do you perfift in faying you will accept my gift?

Mifs PLAYFUL.

Gladly ! I wifh I had more for my friends.

FAIRY.

You would not think how often my offers of this kind are rejected : people love not to be reminded of their faults ; becaufe they are too proud to confefs, and too indolent to correct them.

THE END.